Go to **www.av2books.com**, and enter this book's unique code.

BOOK CODE

W 2 7 3 4 6 8

AV² by Weigl brings you media enhanced books that support active learning.

First Published by

VipoLand Incorporated
32nd East Street No 3-32,
City of Panama,
Republic of Panama

Published by AV² by Weigl
350 5th Avenue, 59th Floor New York, NY 10118
Website: www.av2books.com

Library of Congress Control Number: 2015947861

ISBN: 978-1-4896-3902-8 (hardcover)
ISBN: 978-1-4896-3903-5 (single user eBook)
ISBN: 978-1-4896-3904-2 (multi-user eBook)

Editor: Katie Gillespie
Project Coordinator: Alexis Roumanis
Art Director: Terry Paulhus

Printed in the United States of America in Brainerd, Minnesota
1 2 3 4 5 6 7 8 9 0 19 18 17 16 15

082015
100715

MORAL OF THE STORY

For thousands of years, parents and teachers have used memorable stories called fables to teach simple moral lessons to children.

In the Vipo by AV² series, three friends travel to different countries around the world. They help people learn many important life lessons.

In *Vipo Visits the Tour de France*, Vipo and his friends teach a cyclist to play fairly. The cyclist learns that when he cheats, he is only cheating himself.

This AV² media enhanced book comes alive with...

Animated Video
Watch a custom animated movie.

Try This!
Complete activities and hands-on experiments.

Key Words
Study vocabulary, and complete a matching word activity.

Quiz
Test your knowledge.

Why should you play fairly?

AV² Storytime Navigation

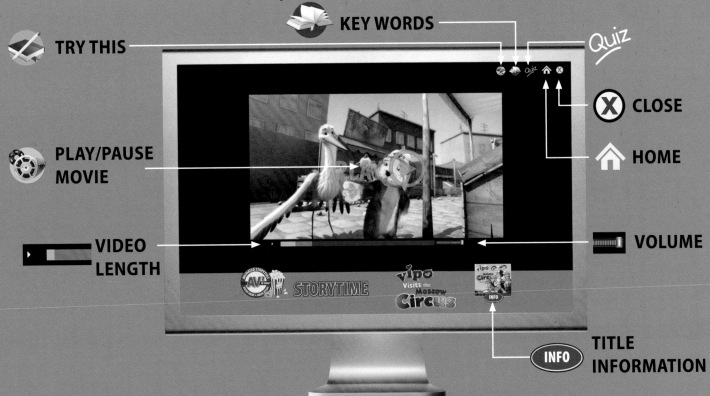

KEY WORDS

TRY THIS

PLAY/PAUSE MOVIE

VIDEO LENGTH

Quiz

X CLOSE

HOME

VOLUME

INFO   TITLE INFORMATION

3

The Characters

Vipo
I am a flying dog.
I travel with my friends
to different places. I am
the leader of our group.

5

The Story

Vipo, Henry, and Betty were flying over Paris, France.

"Look at that tall tower," said Betty.

"It's called the Eiffel Tower," said Henry.

"It's beautiful!" said Betty.

Suddenly, they heard two men shouting at each other.

"Let's see what they are arguing about," said Vipo.

"I'm going to win the race, Pierre!" shouted a man.

"I won't let you, Bernard!" replied Pierre.

"Why are you arguing?" asked Vipo.

"Bernard is trying to win the race by cheating," said Pierre.

"What race?" asked Betty.

"We are racing in the Tour de France," said Pierre.

"I've always wanted to see a cycling race," said Betty.

"Let's go watch it," said Vipo.

The three friends flew to the top of a building.
"This is a great spot to watch the race," said Betty.
"Look," pointed Henry. "Here come some cyclists."
"Can anyone see Pierre and Bernard?" asked Betty.
"There's Bernard," said Vipo.
"Why did he get off his bike?" asked Henry.

Bernard was throwing oil all over the road.

"What is he doing?" asked Betty.

"He's making the road slippery," said Vipo.

"But why?" asked Henry.

"To stop all of those cyclists," said Vipo.

A group of cyclists slid when they ran over the oil.

"Oh no!" cried Betty. "They're all going to fall down."

"That will slow them down," laughed Bernard.

Bernard got back onto his bike.

"What does he have in his hand?" asked Betty.

"They look like thumbtacks," said Henry.

"Oh no!" cried Betty. "He threw them on the road."

The thumbtacks popped the tire of a cyclist.

"Look!" shouted Vipo. "Here comes Pierre."

"We should warn him," exclaimed Betty.

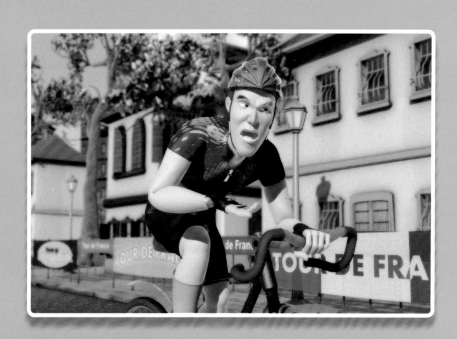

15

"Watch out, Pierre!" shouted Betty.

Vipo flew right behind Pierre.

"There are thumbtacks on the road!" cried Vipo.

Pierre swerved to avoid the thumbtacks.

"Phew!" gasped Pierre. "That was close."

"You can catch Bernard," encouraged Vipo.

Pierre peddled his bike faster.

Just then, Bernard threw more oil onto the road.

"Don't worry," said Vipo. "You can jump over it."

Pierre pulled up on his bike and jumped high into the air.

Pierre jumped so high that he surprised Bernard.

"Oh no!" cried Bernard. "I dropped the oil bottle."

Bernard slipped on the oil and fell over.

"You shouldn't cheat, Bernard!" cried Pierre.

19

Pierre was the first to cross the finish line.

"You did it!" cried Betty.

"You won the Tour de France," said Henry.

A gold medal was placed around Pierre's neck.

"I can't believe it," said Pierre. "I won!"

"I should have won," sobbed Bernard.

"It's best to play fairly," said Vipo.

"But why didn't cheating work for me?" asked Bernard.

"When you cheat, you are only cheating yourself," said Vipo.
"When you're focused on cheating, your attention is not on the race," said Pierre.
"You're right," said Bernard. "Thank you for teaching me an important lesson."

21

Moral of the Story

It is best to play fairly.
When you cheat,
you are only cheating yourself.

Vipo Visits the TOUR DE FRANCE

Quiz

1 Where does the story take place?

2 What was the name of the tall tower?

3 What popped the cyclist's tire?

4 Why did Bernard fall off his bike?

5 Who won the Tour de France?

6 What was given to the winner of the Tour de France?

Answers:
1. Paris
2. The Eiffel Tower
3. A thumbtack
4. He slipped on oil
5. Pierre
6. A gold medal

Check out www.av2books.com for your animated storytime media enhanced book!

1 Go to www.av2books.com

2 Enter book code W 2 7 3 4 6 8

3 Fuel your imagination online!

www.av2books.com

AV² Storytime Navigation

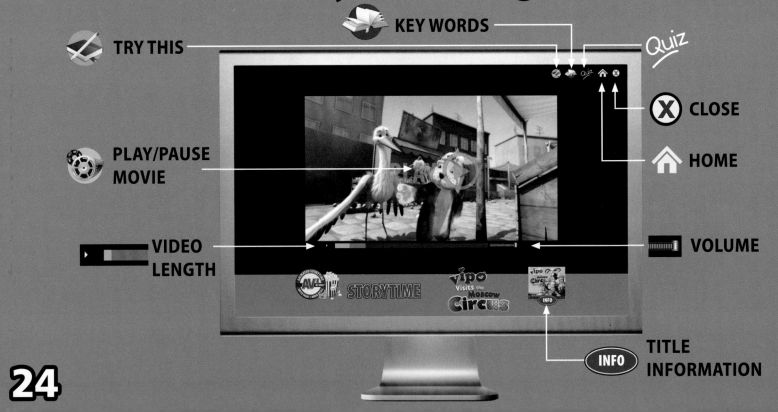

TRY THIS

KEY WORDS

Quiz

X CLOSE

PLAY/PAUSE MOVIE

HOME

VIDEO LENGTH

VOLUME

INFO TITLE INFORMATION